MERCURY
and the
WOODSMAN

Why should you always be honest?

www.av2books.com

Go to **www.av2books.com**, and
enter this book's unique code.

BOOK CODE

S 2 4 4 5 3 6

AV² by Weigl brings you media enhanced
books that support active learning.

Published by AV² by Weigl
350 5th Avenue, 59th Floor New York, NY 10118
Websites: www.av2books.com   www.weigl.com

Library of Congress Cataloging-in-Publication Data

Mercury and the workmen / Aesop.
     pages cm. -- (Storytime)
  Summary: "In Mercury and the Workmen, Aesop and his
troupe teach their audience that honest actions are often
rewarded. They learn that acting honestly gains more
respect than acting dishonestly"-- Provided by publisher.
  ISBN 978-1-4896-2434-5 (hardcover : alk. paper) -- ISBN
978-1-4896-2435-2 (single user ebook) --
ISBN 978-1-4896-2436-9 (multi user ebook)
  [1. Fables. 2. Folklore.] I. Aesop.
  PZ8.2.M46 2014
  398.2--dc23
  [E]
                                    2014009677

Printed in the United States in North Mankato, Minnesota
1 2 3 4 5 6 7 8 9 0 18 17 16 15 14

052014
WEP090514

FABLE SYNOPSIS

For thousands of years, parents and teachers
have used memorable stories called fables to
teach simple moral lessons to children.

In the Aesop's Fables by AV² series, classic
fables are given a lighthearted twist. These
familiar tales are performed by a troupe of
animal players whose endearing personalities
bring the stories to life.

In *Mercury and the Woodsman*, Aesop and his troupe teach their audience that
honest actions are often rewarded. They learn that acting honestly gains more
respect than acting dishonestly.

This AV² media enhanced book comes alive with...

Animated Video
Watch a custom animated movie.

Try This!
Complete activities and hands-on experiments.

Key Words
Study vocabulary, and complete a matching word activity.

Quiz
Test your knowledge.

MERCURY and the WOODSMAN

Why should you always be honest?

AV² Storytime Navigation

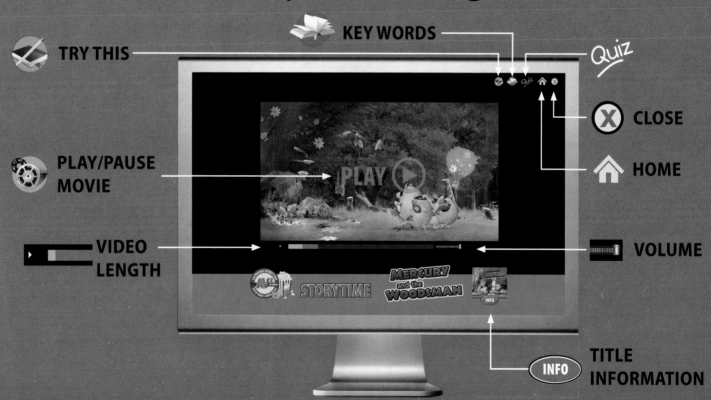

TRY THIS

KEY WORDS

Quiz

CLOSE

PLAY/PAUSE MOVIE

HOME

VIDEO LENGTH

VOLUME

TITLE INFORMATION

INFO

The Players

Aesop
I am the leader of Aesop's Theater, a screenwriter, and an actor.
I can be hot-tempered, but I am also soft and warm-hearted.

Libbit
I am an actor and a prop man.
I think I should have been a lion, but I was born a rabbit.

Presy
I am the manager of Aesop's Theater.
I am also the narrator of the plays.

The Story

Aesop hummed as he crossed a beautiful pond.

"It's been a long time since I had a quiet day."

He thought it would be a great time to write a new play.

Aesop sat down to write.

He did not know what he would write about.

At that moment, he heard the Shorties.

They were arguing with each other.

The Shorties saw Aesop and ran over to him.

"I forgot to pack my lunch," said Audrey.

"Only Goddard remembered to pack his lunch," continued Elvis.

"If I share, I won't have enough to eat!" said Goddard.

Aesop took out his lunch to share with everyone.

"If I share my lunch," said Aesop.

"Will you share your lunch, Goddard?"

Goddard agreed.

"Thank you!" said Bogart. "We were going to starve!"

When they were finished, the Shorties

left for an afternoon nap.

Aesop started to write his play again.

"I don't like what I've written," said Aesop.

He threw the paper, and it hit the back of a raccoon.

"Did you throw this paper at me?" asked the raccoon.

"No!" said Aesop. "It must have been one of the Shorties."

The raccoon uncrumpled the paper and saw that it was Aesop's.

"I don't like it when people litter and lie about it!" said the raccoon.

Aesop felt bad. It gave him a good idea for a new play.

That night, Aesop put on a play for all of the forest animals.

"Welcome to Aesop's Theater!" said Presy.

"Mercury and the Woodsman will be shown today."

One day, a woodsman was cutting down trees by a pond.

The woodsman dropped his axe into the pond by mistake.

The pond was very deep.

The woodsman could not find his axe.

Suddenly, the god Mercury appeared above the pond.

"What happened?" asked Mercury.

"I lost my axe!" said the woodsman.

Mercury dove into the pond and came back with a golden axe.

"Is this yours?" he asked.

"No," said the woodsman.

Mercury went back into the pond.

This time, he came up with a silver axe.

"Then, is this yours?"

"No," said the woodsman. "Mine is made of iron."

19

Mercury dove back into the pond.

He came back with an iron axe.

"Is this yours?" asked Mercury.

"Yes. You've found it!"

"I will reward you for your honesty." said Mercury.

"I will give you the gold, silver, and iron axes."

The woodsman went home with all three axes.

A group of greedy woodsmen heard the story about the golden axe.

They went to the pond where Mercury had appeared.

"If we drop our axes on purpose,

Mercury will give us a golden axe."

They threw their axes into the pond.

Mercury quickly appeared above the pond.

"Did you lose your axes?" he asked.

The woodsmen nodded, and Mercury showed them a golden axe.

"Is this your axe?" asked Mercury.

"It's ours, it's ours!" shouted the woodsmen.

"Where is the silver axe?" asked one of the woodsmen.

The greed of the woodsmen angered Mercury.

"You lied to me. Now, none of you shall have your axes."

After the play, the raccoon found Aesop.

"Aesop, I have looked up the law of the forest.

You owe a fine for littering and lying about it."

Aesop knew he should not have lied to the raccoon.

He felt bad about throwing away a piece of paper.

Aesop paid the fine and said goodbye to the raccoon.

To earn the respect of others, you should always be honest.

What is a Story?

Players

Who is the story about? The characters, or players, are the people, animals, or objects that perform the story. Characters have personality traits that contribute to the story. Readers understand how a character fits into the story by what the character says and does, what others say about the character, and how others treat the character.

Setting

Where and when do the events take place? The setting of a story helps readers visualize where and when the story is taking place. These details help to suggest the mood or atmosphere of the story. A setting is usually presented briefly, but it explains whether the story is taking place in the past, present, or future and in a large or small area.

Plot

What happens in the story? The plot is a story's plan of action. Most plots follow a pattern. They begin with an introduction and progress to the rising action of events. The events lead to a climax, which is the most exciting moment in the story. The resolution is the falling action of events. This section ties up loose ends so that readers are not left with unanswered questions. The story ends with a conclusion that brings the events to a close.

Point of View

Who is telling the story? The story is normally told from the point of view of the narrator, or storyteller. The narrator can be a main character or a less important character in the story. He or she can also be someone who is not in the story but is observing the action. This observer may be impartial or someone who knows the thoughts and feelings of the characters. A story can also be told from different points of view.

Dialogue

What type of conversation occurs in the story? Conversation, or dialogue, helps to show what is happening. It also gives information about the characters. The reader can discover what kinds of people they are by the words they say and how they say them. Writers use dialogue to make stories more interesting. In dialogue, writers imitate the way real people speak, so it is written differently than the rest of the story.

Theme

What is the story's underlying meaning? The theme of a story is the topic, idea, or position that the story presents. It is often a general statement about life. Sometimes, the theme is stated clearly. Other times, it is suggested through hints.

MERCURY and the WOODSMAN Quiz

1 What did Aesop share with the Shorties?

2 What did the Shorties do after lunch?

3 Why was the raccoon mad?

4 What did Mercury show the woodsman first?

5 Why did the woodsman get all three axes?

6 Why did the woodsmen lose their axes?

Answers:
1. His lunch
2. Took a nap
3. Aesop littered and lied.
4. A gold axe
5. He was honest.
6. They lied

Key Words

Research has shown that as much as 65 percent of all written material published in English is made up of 300 words. These 300 words cannot be taught using pictures or learned by sounding them out. They must be recognized by sight. This book contains 116 common sight words to help young readers improve their reading fluency and comprehension. This book also teaches young readers several important content words, such as proper nouns. These words are paired with pictures to aid in learning and improve understanding.

Page	Sight Words First Appearance
4	a, also, am, an, and, be, been, but, can, have, I, of, plays, should, the, think, was
5	always, animals, at, do, food, from, get, good, if, like, never, other, them, to, very, want, with
6	as, day, great, had, he, it's, it, long, new, thought, time, would, write
8	about, did, down, each, him, know, not, over, saw, that, they, were, what
11	eat, enough, for, his, left, my, only, out, said, took, we, when, will, you
13	again, asked, back, don't, idea, me, must, no, one, paper, people, started, this
15	all, night, on, put
17	by, could, find, trees
19	above, came, into, is, made, then, up, went
20	found, give, home, three
23	group, our, story, their, us, where
25	your
26	after, away

Page	Content Words First Appearance
4	actor, leader, lion, manager, narrator, prop man, rabbit, screenwriter, theater
5	dance, music, pig
6	pond
11	afternoon, lunch
13	raccoon
15	forest, mercury, woodsman
17	axe, pond
19	god, golden, iron, silver
23	woodsmen
26	law

Check out av2books.com for your animated storytime media enhanced book!

1 Go to av2books.com

2 Enter book code   S 2 4 4 5 3 6

3 Fuel your imagination online!

www.av2books.com

AV² Storytime Navigation

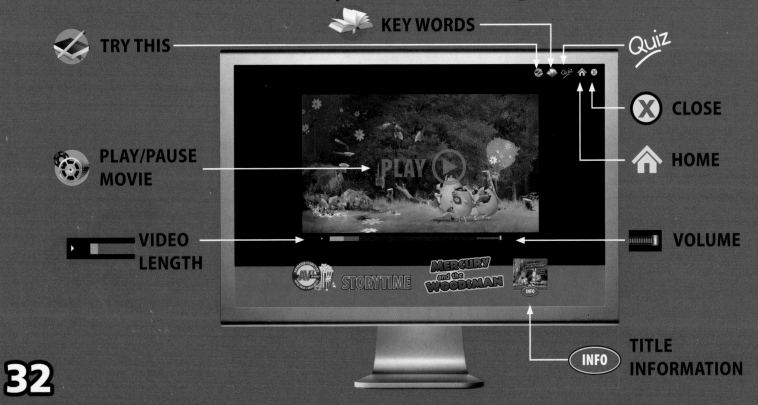

TRY THIS

KEY WORDS

Quiz

PLAY/PAUSE MOVIE

CLOSE

HOME

VIDEO LENGTH

VOLUME

TITLE INFORMATION